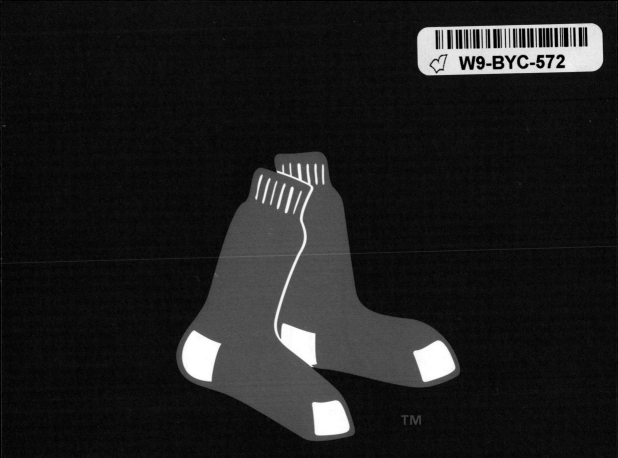

TM

Hello, Wally!

Jerry Remy

Illustrated by Danny Moore

MASCOT BOOKS®
www.mascotbooks.com

It was a beautiful fall day in New England.
Wally The Green Monster was on his way to
Fenway Park for a Boston Red Sox game.

As Wally walked down Yawkey Way,
Red Sox fans cheered,
"Hello, Wally!"

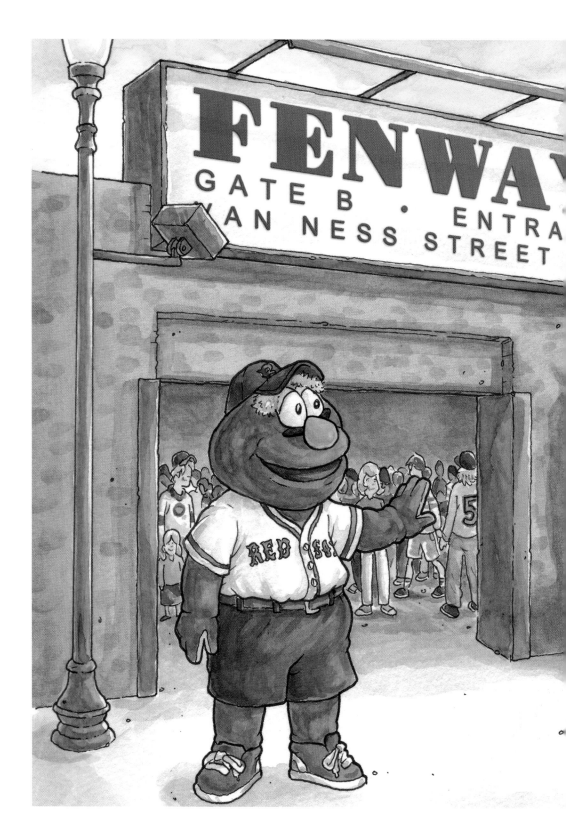

Wally stopped at the statue of Ted Williams,
one of the greatest hitters that ever lived.

As fans admired the statue,
they waved, "Hello, Wally!"

Wally arrived at the ballpark in time for batting practice. The Red Sox took batting practice in their red jerseys.

As the team's best hitter stepped
to home plate, he said, "Hello, Wally!"

After batting practice, the Fenway Park
grounds crew proudly prepared
the field for play.

As the grounds crew worked,
they cheered, "Hello, Wally!"

Wally was feeling hungry. He grabbed a
few snacks and a Red Sox pennant at
the concession stand.

As he made his way back to the field,
a family cheered, "Hello, Wally!"

It was now time to introduce the Red Sox team. The team was dressed in their classic white uniforms and navy blue caps.

Wally ran onto the field waving a Red Sox
flag. The crowd cheered, "Hello, Wally!"

The umpire yelled, "Play Ball!"
After a perfect first pitch,
the umpire called, "Strike One!"

With the game underway, Wally admired
beautiful Fenway Park. He felt proud to
be a part of the Red Sox family.

The Red Sox batted in a run. Wally
watched the scoreboard operator change
the score on the Green Monster™ wall.

The scoreboard operator spotted Wally
in the bleachers and yelled,
"Hello, Wally!"

It was now time for the seventh inning
stretch. The organ player played
"Take Me Out To The Ballgame!"™

Wally led the crowd in song. Afterwards,
Red Sox fans cheered, "Hello, Wally!"

With the game tied in the ninth inning,
a Red Sox player hit the ball over
the Green Monster wall. Home run!

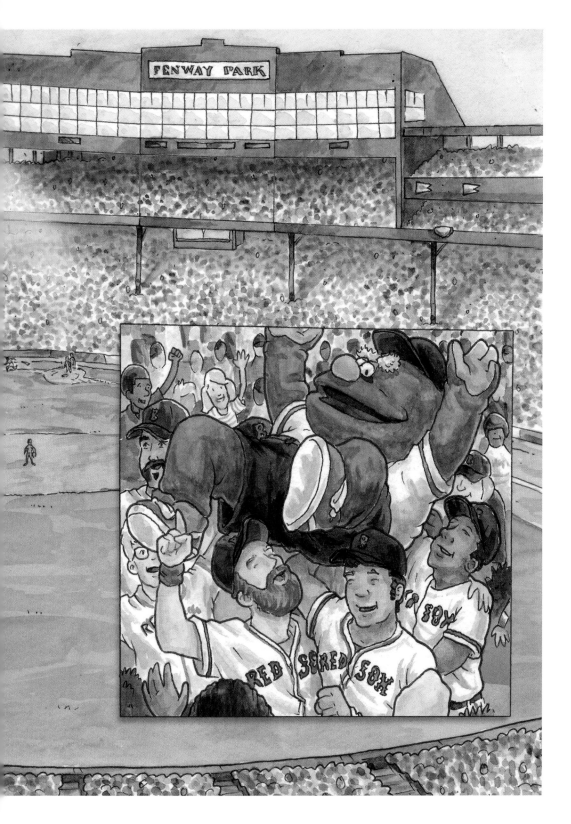

The team gathered around home plate
to celebrate the victory.
The team cheered, "Red Sox win, Wally!"

After the game, Wally headed to his
home inside the Green Monster wall.

Wally was tired and fell fast asleep.
Good night, Wally!

To my favorite Wally fan, my grandson, Dominik. ~ Jerry Remy

This one goes out to the Hultwelkers,
especially Mike, Pete, and Dewey. ~ Danny Moore

Special thanks to:

Christopher Bergstrom - Boston Red Sox
John O'Rourke
Trisha Saintelus-Curtis
Don Hintze
Maria Montoya
Brandon Cook

For more information about our products, please visit us online at www.mascotbooks.com.

Mascot Books, Inc.
P.O. Box 220157
Chantilly, VA 20153-0157

Major League Baseball trademarks and copyrights are used
with permission of Major League Baseball Properties, Inc.

ISBN: 1-932888-80-2

Printed in the United States.

www.mascotbooks.com